I0520003

ORPHAN OLLIE OPTS OUT

Mario E. Lombardo

This book is a work of fiction. Any resemblance to actual events or persons, living or dead, is entirely coincidental.

"Orphan Ollie Opts Out," by Mario E. Lombardo. ISBN 978-1-63868-163-2 (softcover).

Published 2024 by Virtualbookworm.com Publishing Inc., P.O. Box 9949, College Station, TX 77842, US.
©2024, Mario E. Lombardo. All rights reserved. No part of this publication may be reproduced, stored in a retrieval system, or transmitted in any form or by any means, electronic, mechanical, recording or otherwise, without the prior written permission of Mario E. Lombardo.

SPECIAL THANKS

To Lisa L. Drew and Ralph S. Martini for their valued insights and suggestions and to Caroline Ann Rubino for subtitles "Love on Cordova Street" and "Aisle Seat, 3rd Row. Left, Orchestra"

DEDICATION

To the more than 100,000 children in United States waiting for adoption.

1.

I collapsed in a kitchen chair, mentally and physically exhausted, and took a long deep breath. It was finally over, the neighbors all gone. They tidied up the place before leaving and my best friend's mom told me that she and Christopher, her husband, would stop over in the morning to talk a little about the future.

The future, what future, I thought. I'm sixteen and all alone. What is going to happen to me? And why did Mom have to suddenly die. It's just not fair. The two of us were doing fine. I was enjoying 10th grade and Mom liked her cashier job at the neighborhood grocery store. We were making a go of it. Tears started to stream down my face and I sobbed uncontrollably until I fell asleep.

The next morning Luke's parents, Mr. and Mrs. Armenti, came over as promised and discussed what would happen next. They had contacted the local Child Services Agency and were told that I would receive a visit this very afternoon from someone from that office who would interview me and answer any questions I had.

That afternoon, as expected, Ms. Catelin, a social worker from the Agency, stopped by and asked a bunch of questions. My age, height, weight, school grade, and interests, all of which she dutifully wrote down in a notebook. She then told me Mr. Goldman would visit tomorrow morning to lay out all available options for placement, answer questions, and record my preferences. She took a couple of photos, wished me good luck, and then left.

My head was spinning, things were all happening too fast. I was both confused and scared and thought I had better start thinking about what to do. I'm not sure I wanted some strangers mapping out my life.

Luke stopped by later and said that he overheard his parents talking about adopting me. He said he loved the idea that we could become brothers. Wow, I told him, I am really getting confused about the lightning speed of what's happening. I told him that I needed to think things over a bit. Luke understood and asked me to not do anything rash, and to hear what the State Agency folks had to say before deciding anything.

I tossed and turned in bed that night, awakening when I heard a loud knocking on the door. I jumped up, slipped on a pair of jeans, and let Mr. Goldman in. He was a pleasant man who informed me about available options, including adoption, a foster home, or an all-boys orphanage. I had seen movies about life in foster homes and orphanages and was not sure that I wanted any part of those places. And, as for Mr. and Mrs. Armenti and Luke, they were a nice, respectable family, and I was thankful for their kindness but I just didn't feel right about it for some reason.

The next day, a $2,000 insurance check arrived in the mail. So, I thought, why not? I am sixteen, tall for my age, confident and smart, and have $2,000 for food and rent. Yes, I would catch the next Greyhound bus to warm, sunny Florida. I would opt out on my own.

2.

The teller at the bank asked if I wanted to open a savings or checking account and I said that I would take the proceeds in cash. She cautioned against doing that but sensed I was determined so she placed the money in a thick bank envelope and handed it to me. I picked up my small suitcase and left for the bus station.

The ticket agent at the Greyhound terminal informed me only one seat was available. I bought it and walked to the end of a long line of passengers waiting for the bus driver to open the door for boarding. There was a lot of talking and noisy commotion upon boarding with passengers stopping by their seats, tossing their baggage into the storage bins above and banging the bin-doors shut. When I found my seat in the rear of the bus, I tossed my small suitcase in the storage bin above, and an older man stepped out in the aisle signaling me with his hand that I was to sit in the window seat. After settling in, I quickly opened up a paperback I had bought at the terminal and started to read. I didn't want to get involved in a conversation with a stranger.

All was fine for about the first hour, the bus rolling southward from Savannah. I closed my book, leaned against the window, and shut my eyes to relax. The stress of the morning activities tired me a little and before long I was napping. Some time later I awakened, and thought I smelled alcohol. Sensing that I did, my seat mate quickly leaned over to me and in a whispering voice said he was medicating under doctor's orders and hoped that I didn't mind that he had to take a sip of his medicine periodically. His medicine was concealed in a small brown paper bag that he kept in the pocket of the seat in front of him. It smelled like alcohol to me, but not really knowing what to do about it, I lied and said I understood and didn't mind at all.

Another hour passed and our bus driver announced that we were arriving at the Florida Welcome Center where we would be stopping for a break. He invited us to see him if we had any questions, reminded us to secure our personal items, and cautioned that the bus would depart in exactly one-half hour. Upon hearing his remark about personal items, I quickly felt the front of my sweater to check on my hidden bank envelope. I had tucked it under my belt for safekeeping. I felt nothing. I panicked, looked immediately at my seat mate, and questioned him about it in a somewhat accusatory tone of voice. He calmly said he would help me look for it, got on his knees, and then pointed his finger at something on the floor under our seat. The "something" turned out to be my missing bank envelope.

My best guess was it slipped out when I stretched upwards, hands over head, to deposit my suitcase in the bin and didn't hear it fall because of all of the noise in the bus at that time. I sheepishly thanked my seat mate and hurried off the bus red-faced, knowing I reacted like a stupid jerk over the incident.

As I walked toward the Center's restroom, I noticed a state trooper talking to our bus driver. While washing my hands in the restroom I overheard two passengers saying that the trooper was looking for a youngster who was reported missing by the Savannah Child Service Agency and was believed to be heading South on a bus. I hurried out of the Center's rear door and spotted a small pickup truck with a tarp stretched over its bed, loosened some of its fasteners, climbed in, and secured the tarp. My heart was thumping as I laid down on the metal floor-bed and waited. Minutes later, I heard the front door of the truck slam, the engine turn over, and felt the truck beginning to move.

3.

After an hour or so, I felt the truck leave the highway and come to a stop. I heard the driver get out and walk away so I peeked out from under the tarp and saw him going into the door of the Shell gas station. I scrambled out, hurried into an on-site McDonald's and bought a cheeseburger, fries, and a soda. I asked the clerk the name of the town and she said Jacksonville. I smiled, thanked her, sat, and decided my next move while gulping down my food. I knew St Augustine was near, about a couple of hours away at most. My Mom and I had visited the city one summer and we loved it.

Then I caught my first break. A young couple leaving the station saw me hitchhiking and asked where I was going. They told me to hop in the back, that they would be driving through St Augustine on their way to Daytona. They asked if I lived there and I lied and said I was visiting my Aunt and Uncle there. "Well," the wife asked, "why were you in Jacksonville and where is your luggage or backpack." I lied again saying that I was on the Greyhound going to St Augustine but somehow I lost track of the time and it left without me and it had my luggage. "Oh," she sympathized, "you poor young man." "It will be okay" added her husband, "you can fetch it at the depot in St Augustine when we drop you off." "Yeah, I'll certainly do that" I replied and then I leaned back into my seat and for the first time all day breathed easily and relaxed.

I was dropped off at the Bridge of Lions as the couple continued southward to Daytona. It was nearing five o'clock so I checked in one of the nearby motels lining the street overlooking the Matanzas Bay. I then left to reacquaint myself with the city. I saw one street sign with an arrow pointing to Fort Matanzas and another pointing to St Augustine Beach.

Not today, I thought, I only had about an hour until nightfall so I spent it walking the streets of the Historic District. I saw Flagler College, many attractive small grassy parks with welcoming palm trees and benches, and a Burger King, where I bought a couple of whoppers, fries, and shake to go. I was tired and decided to return to the motel to eat, shower, watch a little TV, then catch some sleep. On my way back I passed the Cathedral Basilica and remembered my Mom and I attending mass there during our visit. I tried the front door, it was open, so I entered, knelt in a pew facing the altar, saw a statue of Blessed Mother Mary and asked her to please take care of my Mom and to tell her I missed her very much, but was doing okay.

4.

I awoke early, got the location of Greyhound station from the motel clerk, and headed to Cordova Street. After picking up my suitcase, I headed back to the Basilica. I knocked on the door of the rectory and a stern, elderly lady led me into a small room where I sat and waited as instructed. About five minutes later, a priest arrived and greeted me. "I'm Father Gatto, the pastor here, how can I help you?" I told him my name, that I arrived last evening from Georgia, and that I needed a job. I lied and told him I had graduated high school and was 18. Lying was bad enough but lying to a priest surely earned me a "Going to Hell" card---but I felt I had no choice. I knew I needed to be eighteen to get a job. We talked for about a half hour and Father said he would see what he could do and that I should stop back on Wednesday at one o'clock. I thanked him and left.

I returned to the motel, changed into fresh clothes, and headed out to try my luck in finding a job. I stopped in some local clothing shops, couple of restaurants, and at the college, all without success. It seemed that the local college students filled most of the entry-level jobs in the area.

That evening in my motel room, I opened the thick bank envelope and counted my money. $1,580. Yes, I definitely needed to find a job soon.

So, the next morning, I stopped off at the rectory to see Father Gatto. I apologized for bothering him a day earlier than agreed but stressed I was getting a little nervous about my financial situation. Father Gatto smiled and said I was in luck, that he didn't know how to contact me to tell me the good news---that I was to drop by and see Mr. Martini at his pizza shop. He gave me the address, I thanked him, and dashed off.

The "Mom and Pop Pizza Shop" was a small pizza carryout place in a cobbled-street near the college. It occupied the first-floor front of a small bungalow. Mr. Martini, the owner, looked over the one-page application he asked me to fill out, asked a few questions, and told me he would hire me on a trial basis. Wow, I couldn't believe my ears. My very first job. He told me to report in the morning at 10. Prep work had to be done, he said, before we opened the door at 11:00.

My first week at the shop flew by. I enjoyed working with Mr. M. He was patient, fair, and complimentary of my attitude and hustle. We were developing into an efficient team. I was responsible for taking the orders, handing the boxed pizzas to customers, and operating the cash register. Mr. M made the pizzas and boxed them. He was a whiz at both. I also learned Mrs. Martini had died of cancer last year and Father Gatto had befriended him since her funeral mass.

5.

I rented a room at a nearby YMCA to cut my expenses, opened a checking account at the local Wells Fargo Bank and was feeling optimistic about things. I stopped at the Basilica after work on occasion and asked Blessed Mary to tell my Mom I had a job working with a very nice man, and that I think about her every night as I lay in bed.

As the weeks rolled by, I fell into a comfortable rhythm working with Mr. M. Our work relationship was spilling over into a personal one. He invited me over for dinner on Sunday after mass, then the next Sunday we went fishing at the pier, then the beach the Sunday after. I enjoyed his company and he seemed to enjoy mine. Business was thriving. Pizza sales were spurting upwards week after week. Mr. M often kidded me about the sudden spike in young teeny-bopper traffic, especially Rosie

Fernandez, the cute high-schooler who seemed to stop by the shop quite often after school. When I asked Mr. M how he knew her name, he said that St Augustine was a small town and everyone pretty much knew everyone, that he knew the Fernandez family from Church. Months whizzed by. I was happy while at work, but truth be told, I got lonely at night in my room. I missed my Mom. I even missed attending school with my friends and my teacher, Miss Caroline. And, of course, my best friend Luke. I vowed that when I turned eighteen I would return to Savannah to see them.

The next morning, as usual, I popped out of bed and hurried off to work. When I got there, I saw a policeman inside talking with Mr. M. My heart stopped. The policeman asked me my name and I told him. He then said I was wanted by a Child Service Agency in Savannah, that I was only seventeen and still a Ward of the State of Georgia, and that Mr. Goldman would be arriving tomorrow by auto to take me back to Savannah. When he said my age aloud, Mr. M. looked at me and said "Ollie, I am so disappointed in you, you didn't tell me the truth, and I trusted you." I said I was so sorry and could explain but Mr. M was visibly upset, shook his head from side to side, turned around, and walked back into the storeroom. The policeman cautioned me to pack up my things and to be ready to go with Mr. Goldman tomorrow morning at 9. He and Mr. Goldman would meet me at the front desk of the Y.

I tossed and turned that night in bed feeling sad and bad about lying to Mr. M. I talked to my Mom, told her about the trouble I was in, and asked for her help. The alarm awakened me at 7. I showered, dressed, and packed my things. I took the elevator down to the main floor and waited for Mr. Goldman to arrive.

The policeman arrived about a half hour later and then Mr. Goldman showed up at 9. Also coming through the door was Mr. M, Father Gatto, and another gentleman carrying a briefcase. The adults huddled in a small room off the lobby. I wondered what was happening and was nervous. When they came back out, Mr. Goldman informed me that Mr. M's attorney was prepared to immediately initiate the necessary legal paperwork for adoption. That Mr. Martini wanted to adopt me as his son, if I was receptive. I looked over to Mr. M and he looked back at me with tears in his eyes as he spread his arms wide. Mr. Goldman looked at me and asked "Well?" I yelled "Yes" and flung myself into Mr. M's open arms and embraced him in a long, tight hug. I was sobbing with happiness.

"My mother would have loved you, Mr. Martini" I blurted out.

"And Mrs. Martini would have loved you, Ollie," he replied.

ODE TO HUMANITY.

On purpose no surname has Ollie in this story
his processing of grief, loneliness, and fears galore
mirror those of orphans everywhere
hoping Humanity will hurry
with offers of heartfelt love to be alone no more.

II.
OLLIE AND ROSIE
LOVE ON CORDOVA STREET

1.

The school bell rang and Rosie Fernandez gathered her books and headed out the door. It was Friday and she would be heading off to the Mom and Pop Pizza Shop to enjoy her customary TGIF slice of pizza and to see the handsome young man behind the counter, Ollie Martini.

Rosie was a senior at St Augustine High and has had a crush on Ollie since her junior year. She and Ollie had not really said much to each other. She would say "Hi", order a slice of plain cheese pizza from him, and take it outside and sit on the bench across the cobbled-street from the shop. She sat there on purpose knowing he could see her from the huge shop window. She knew Ollie was a teenage orphan from Georgia who had been adopted by Mr. Martini, a widower, who owned the pizza shop. Every family who attended the Cathedral Basilica had heard about that special event. Father Gatto even worked the news of the adoption into the text of one of his Sunday homilies. That is part of the charm of the small-town feel of St Augustine, everyone seemed instantly to know any special news or happenings of the day.

Rosie liked the fact that Ollie was not a local and, therefore, probably not aware that she was not a U.S. citizen. Growing up, she was sometimes made to feel embarrassed by that fact. Her mom and dad had emigrated from Mexico when she was a year old. She was so looking forward to her 18th birthday when she could initiate the naturalization process to become a citizen. Both of her parents had become naturalized citizens and were doing fine. Her father was employed as a heavy-machine operator for the Park Service, and her mom as a short-order chef at the local Flagler College.

On this pleasant Friday afternoon, an auspicious event happened. Not being busy, Ollie told Mr. M that he was going to step outside for a minute or two to chat with Rosie. Over the past year, Ollie and Rosie often had exchanged a few pleasantries in the shop and after mass on Sunday, but nothing more. But Ollie knew he liked what he saw and heard and was ready to ask her out. He had remarked to Mr. M that he probably was the only seventeen-year old in St

Augustine who had never dated. As for Rosie, although she was well-liked at school, cute, and smart enough to make the Honor Roll, she also had never dated. The two of them quickly relaxed upon sharing that news and chatted nonstop as if they had known each other since birth. They agreed to see a movie this coming Sunday at the Corazon theatre. Rosie gave Ollie her phone number and address before departing. The Mom and Pop Pizza Shop had a newly arriving customer and Ollie had to return to work.

Ollie was anxious to see her again and felt Sunday would never arrive. Five blocks away, in her family's three-bedroom apartment on Orange Street, Rosie Fernandez was similarly wondering why it was taking so long for Sunday to arrive.

2.

Mr. M dropped Ollie off at Rosie's place at 5. (Ollie had a Florida driver license but Mr. M would not let him drive his 2005 Hyundai Sonata until he was 18.) Ollie rang the bell and Rosie answered the door looking sparkly and pretty. A tiny shockwave rippled through his body when he saw her "You look very nice," he blurted. "Thank you," she replied, then introduced him to her mom, dad, and younger sister and brother. As they started to leave, Mr. Fernandez reminded her that she had school tomorrow and to be home not later than 9.

They walked to the Cordova Street bus stop, hopped on the bus, and headed for the cinema, talking as they walked and sat side-by-side on the bus. After the movie, they stopped at a nearby ice cream shop and indulged in huge hot fudge sundaes. They were laughing as they chatted over the sundaes clearly enjoying each other's company.

When walking to the bus stop to return home, Ollie extended his hand downward near Rosie and she grasped it and gave it a little squeeze. They looked at each other and smiled but said nothing and kept walking hand-in-hand. The bus ride home was pure happiness and joy of two young teenagers, each of whom had found someone special.

When they reached the door of Rosie's home, they faced each other, looked into each others eyes, but Ollie was not sure whether he should kiss her goodnight. He didn't want to rush things and spoil the evening. So, he asked her "Will it be okay if I kiss you?" Rosie, looked at him, nodded her approval, and said "Yes, please do."

When Ollie arrived home, Mr. M asked him if he and Miss Fernandez enjoyed each others company. "Yes," he said. "Then you will probably be seeing her again, I guess," asked Mr. M. Ollie responded again with a monosyllabic "Yes." Mr. M took the hint and said he was going to get ready for bed and left the room. Ollie grabbed a soda from the fridge, sat down in a living room chair, and slowly savored and rehashed everything he and Rosie did on the date. Especially the kiss at the end.

Well, the kiss was Rosie's first and it exhilarated her. She recalled everything about it. His gentle grab of her shoulders, then his lightly pulling her in closer to him until their lips met. It was soft and warm. After which, they looked into each other eyes and they both knew their attraction to each other was rapidly developing beyond mere friendship. Somehow, almost magically, reminisced Rosie, a single, gentle kiss confirmed their relationship had elevated to a romantic one. She held on to that pleasant thought until she fell asleep.

Rosie and Ollie soon became a couple. Talking daily and seeing each other whenever they were both free. On successive Sundays, they biked over the Bridge of Lions to spend the afternoons at Crescent Beach, or visited the local museums, fort, and other historic sites. And on Sunday evenings, they typically saw a movie or caught a play performed by drama students at Flagler College. But mainly they talked.

About everything.

Ollie told her about his mother's unexpected death, his period of grief and loneliness, his decision not to go to a State-sponsored foster home or orphanage, and his reason for selecting St Augustine as his destination. Rosie in turn told Ollie about her early school years and how, at times, some kids would call her ugly names and tease her about her Mexican heritage. She also confided that she was never invited by a boy to a school dance or prom. They comforted each other as they talked.

Not unexpectedly, after months of dating, they began talking about their future plans. Ollie would turn 18 soon and planned on taking the Florida GED exam and then, hopefully, attend Flagler at night. His career goal was to become a successful entrepreneur. Rosie related that she would turn 18 this coming April and also planned on attending college. She was a serious student hoping to obtain a much-needed scholarship or other form of financial aid. Her career goal was to return to her highly-ranked high school to teach English and Literature.

During this committed dating period, their physical embracing occurred more often and their kisses longer, signaling their growing romantic feelings about each other---they were falling in love and getting excited about spending the future together.

3.

Time flew by as it often does with people falling in love.

On Ollie's 18th birthday, Mr. M invited Rosie and her family over for cake and ice cream. Mr. and Mrs. Fernandez, Rosie, and her younger sister Elena and brother Ernest all came. It was a very enjoyable evening and made Rosie and Ollie feel especially good about how the parents supported their close relationship. After singing the traditional Happy Birthday song, Ollie made a wish while looking at Rosie, blew out the candles, and cut the cake. After enjoying cake and ice cream, Rosie gave Ollie his present. It was a nice blue (to match his eyes) Under Armor Jacksonville Jaguars T-shirt, which Ollie immediately modeled to mock applause. But the big surprise of the night occurred when Ollie was presented with a set of keys by Mr. M to his Sonata. Ollie thanked him and immediately announced that he would drive Rosie home, that is, if her parents didn't object.

Splashes of exciting news seemed to be occurring weekly. First, Ollie proudly announced that he passed the Florida GED exam and planned to now take the SATs for college. Rosie, a couple of weeks later, celebrated becoming a U.S. citizen erasing the little black cloud that hovered over her for 18 years of her life. They were pleased at having accomplished the initial goals they had set in planning their future together.

The calendar flipped to May---and Rosie's senior year at St Augustine High was coming to a close. She was ecstatic about going to the school prom with Ollie. It would be her first attendance at a school dance and she was eager to show off Ollie to her friends. For the special event, her parents promised her a fancy prom dress from Michaels. And Ollie would be renting and wearing his first tuxedo and driving the Sonata.

Exciting times, indeed.

Rosie allowed herself to fantasize the prom as a dress rehearsal for her marriage to Ollie when she turned 21. On her 18th birthday, Ollie had surprised her with a silver signet ring with a "21" inscribed on the ring's distinguishable flat top. "Creating a lifetime commitment" he uttered, as he placed the ring on her finger. They were deeply and openly in love. Only time stood in the way of marriage.

It was the Friday before prom weekend and Rosie was anxious to see Ollie to finalize the prom plans. They had talked on the phone every day during the week but both were busy and hadn't seen each other. She packed her books into her knapsack and headed out the door for Cordova Street. She saw her bus and started waving her hands as she ran to flag it down, but the driver failed to see her and kept going. It was a nice day so she decided to walk the 5 blocks rather than wait a half-hour or so for the next bus. As she walked, she visualized Ollie and herself talking and laughing as they sat on "their bench."

A headline in the St Augustine evening paper screamed:

LOCAL PEDESTRIAN HIT BY DRUNK DRIVER

At 3:30 P.M. Friday, St John County police received a call of an accident on Cordova Street. Witnesses saw a Mercedes traveling at a high rate of speed, going over the center median, and striking a pedestrian. The pedestrian, 18-year-old Rosie Fernandez of 314 Orange Street, was rushed by ambulance to St Augustine

Hospital and admitted into the Intensive Care Unit.

The police reported that the blood-alcohol level of the driver of the vehicle, 28-year-old Joan Lalley of Palm Beach, was .368 at the time of the crash. Mrs. Lalley was charged with DUI, endangerment, and possibly manslaughter. Witnesses reported that Ms. Fernandez was hit so hard her body flew up and over the roof of the Mercedes and landed on the street. At the time of this news release, there was no further status of her medical condition from the hospital.

Around 4 o'clock, the phone rang in the Mom and Pop Pizza Shop. Mr. Fernandez informed Ollie that Rosie had been seriously injured in an auto accident and was taken to St Augustine Hospital.

When Mr. M and Ollie arrived at the waiting room of the Intensive Care Unit, Elena and Ernest were sitting beside their mother, as she comforted their crying by gently stroking their heads lying on her lap. Mr. Fernandez shot up from his chair embracing first Mr. M and then Ollie. He informed them that Rosie was undergoing an emergency operation and they were waiting to hear the results from the surgeon.

Not another word was spoken. Mrs. Fernandez began praying the rosary.

4.

They all immediately leaped from their seats as Dr Linarelli, the neurosurgeon, entered the room. His news was unemotional and straight-forward. "The procedure went as well as could be expected. Your daughter is in the recovery room but in very serious condition. We'll know more in the next few hours. I'll keep you informed as soon as I have something further to report." He then left the room as quickly as he arrived.

So, they stoically waited, and waited, as the hours slowly ticked on. Around 7, Elena and Ernest said they were getting hungry so Mrs. Fernandez took them to the hospital cafeteria. When they returned, she looked at her husband's face and knew immediately that the news was not good. He went to her, hugged her tightly, and told her "Mary, our Rosie didn't make it."

"No," she screamed. "I want to see her. Please, Frank, take me to my daughter, I want to see her!" she cried hysterically. Mr. Fernandez pleaded with her to please sit down for a minute. With tears in his eyes, he explained that the massive physical injuries made her unrecognizable and he would never forgive himself if he let her see Rosie in that condition. "Please, Mary, I beg you, you have to trust me, you don't want to remember Rosie that way." He wrapped his arms around her tightly and held her shaking body. They were sobbing uncontrollably.

The funeral mass at the Basilica was packed with adults, teens, and children. Her high school class and teachers were in attendance. So was a large group of men from Council 611, Knights of Columbus, friends of Mr. Fernandez. Also attending were many families of parishioners who knew and respected the Fernandez family.

Rosie's closed coffin was on the altar as the requiem mass began.

Father Gatto began conducting the service and quiet sobbing rippled throughout the church. After the readings from the bible were completed, the good Father offered some brief consoling remarks to the Fernandez family, and then announced that "Ollie Martini would now say a few words."

After first introducing himself, Ollie took a deep breath, collected himself, and began: "Rosie was the first girl I met when I arrived here from Savannah two years ago. We were attracted to each other from the first day we met. (PAUSED TO TAKE A DEEP BREATH) We soon began dating steadily, fell in love, and on her 18th birthday, just last month, we committed to marrying when she reached 21."

Ollie's eyes began tearing and he started to choke up. He reached for the bottle in his back pocket and took a sip of water. Then he continued: "I just want to say to Mr. and Mrs. Fernandez, Elena, and Ernest, that Rosie was a special young lady who filled my heart with happiness and joy and I will treasure every memory she and I shared. I will miss her very much."

The emotional-filled funeral mass was followed by interment at the local San Lorenzo Cemetery. The Catholic ceremonial rite at the cemetery was brief and ended with Father Gatto's recital of a final prayer. As everyone began to depart, Mr. Fernandez approached Ollie, shook his hand, told him he was deeply moved by his personal remarks at mass, and thanked him on behalf of the family. Mrs. Fernandez then embraced Ollie and while doing so placed Rosie's silver signet ring in one of his hands. Seeing the ring, Ollie finally lost his composure and completely broke down.

Mr. M and Ollie rode home without a word spoken. After drinking a glass of water in the kitchen to help control his emotions, Mr. M approached Ollie who was standing and staring out the living room window. He gave him a hug, and told him that he was so proud that he was his son. He then asked how he was holding up.

Ollie, with tears streaming down his face, replied: "I keep wondering, if only she would have caught the bus as usual. I don't know, Dad, first my Mom, and now Rosie. I'm not sure I'm going to make it this time."

ODE TO LOVE AND INNOCENCE

What tragically ended on Cordova Street
was not death of life
but of love of two young souls
of passionate purity and hope
separated by a shadowed mystery
that forever taunts and haunts the heart in
whys

III.
OLLIE AND RUTH
AISLE SEAT, 3RD ROW, LEFT ORCHESTRA

1.

Ollie Martini is now 24.

It has been 6 years since Rosie Fernandez was tragically killed by a drunk driver. Both were 18 at the time, deeply in love, and had planned to marry when she turned 21. Her sudden death left an emotional trail of grief and devastation that Ollie felt almost impossible to deal with. He became severely depressed, needed an extensive period of grief-counseling, and hadn't even considered dating anyone for two years. Fortunately, as the time-honored proverb teaches, "Time heals all broken hearts" and Ollie eventually recovered, graduated from local Flagler College's Business School with honors, and was working tirelessly to fulfill his dream goal of becoming a successful entrepreneur.

After graduation, he channeled all of his time and energy into Mom and Pop Pizza Shop. Pizza sales had plateaued a little so day after day Ollie kept creating different types of new pizza products until finally deciding, with Mr. M's approval, to market test a new creation called the "Tini Two Pack." It consisted of two tiny 4"x4" square pizzas, offered only with mozzarella cheese or veggies, and packaged in an eco-friendly takeout container. The new pizza product was advertised with the slogan: "For a Healthy Snack, Buy a Tini Two Pack."

And buy they did. The Tini Two Pack was a smashing success. Local social media was lighting up with favorable customer feedback. Mom and Pop Pizza Shop was soon operating at full capacity six days a week with, at times, customer lines spilling out the door to the sidewalk. To handle the increased volume of phone orders, two college students from Flagler were hired as new part-time members of the team.

The business was clamoring for expansion. Ollie explored with Mr. M the idea of venturing into the franchising business. Mr. M reminded Ollie that he was 58, looking forward to retirement, and lacked the energy to take on such a huge commitment at his age. After thoroughly exploring alternatives, both agreed it would be more prudent to take a slower path to expansion and to first test the opening of another store.

Ollie's research led him to the Gulf-side city of Sarasota. Sarasota had everything to offer, a fast-growing population, a vibrant economy, a warm and sunny climate, the clear blue water of the Gulf of Mexico with its white sugary-sand beaches, a broad spectrum of restaurants, and multiple offerings of varied cultural amenities.

Mr. M and Ollie agreed that Sarasota lacked only one attraction: the Tini Two Pack. So, they opened their second store on Main Street in Sarasota's bustling downtown area.

They lured their good friends Frank and Mary Fernandez to relocate to Sarasota to manage the new store by matching their current salaries and by offering each of them a too-good-to-resist 10% ownership stake in the business. Mr. M knew Frank and Mary would make perfect business partners. They were hardworking, trustworthy, and reliable. Mary's years of experience as a short order chef in a commercial kitchen was a plus and their selection proved to be a wise choice. The business operated at a profit in its very first week and sales were steadily climbing week after week. Daughter Elena and son Ernest soon joined their parents completing the family team.

Ollie's market research was paying off. The template of the St Augustine business model was working successfully in Sarasota.

2.

Sales and profits of the Tini Two Pac rocketed even higher after receiving an unexpected adrenaline boost from Ollie's appearance on ABC's popular business reality TV show, "Shark Tank". [The Tank's panel of Sharks (investors) first listen to pitches from entrepreneurs seeking funds for their businesses/products and then each Shark decides whether or not to make the capital investment.] The panel loved the taste, size, and healthy ingredients of the Tini Two Pack. Also, its eco-friendly packaging, and its impressive sales numbers and high profit margins. They even agreed that the offering price for a 10% ownership stake in the business was fairly valued.

But, nonetheless, Ollie had no takers, hearing "nothing proprietary about pizza, pizza is pizza" from one Shark, "wishing you the best" passes from others, and a wordy dismissive from the last Shark who remarked "the pizza sales growth is impressive but represents only a temporary blip triggered by the social media endorsement of Stephen King, the famous author, who lives on one of Sarasota's barrier islands."

Ollie disagreed with the Shark's "temporary blip in sales" reference, but said nothing. He graciously thanked the panel and left without a deal.

However, as it sometimes happens, the national TV exposure of Tini Two Pack on the popular Shark Tank show resulted in two nationally-known pizza chains extending purchase offers for the business. One offer was for $5.7 million and the other for $5.9 million.

The four owners were stunned by the amounts offered. They agreed to think about the offers overnight, and to discuss them in the morning. During the morning teleconference, they unanimously agreed to offer the interested buyers an option to purchase the business at a fixed date two years in the future, at a price to be determined by a mutually agreed-upon investment banking firm. The two-year exercise date was the secret sauce of the offer. It was selected to coincide with the long-planned retirements of Mr. M and Mr. Fernandez. To their delight, one of the national chains quickly accepted the offer.

Months flew by as the passage of time was not labored but enjoyed by the every-day rhythm of successful entrepreneurs at work. During the ensuing two-year period, both stores continued their steady growth of quarterly sales and profits.

3.

After his weekly business meetings with Frank and Mary, Ollie would routinely attend a cultural offering at the Asolo Theatre, the Van Wezel Hall, or the Sarasota Opera House, spending the night at the local Ritz-Carlton before returning home in the morning. He enjoyed the performances to such an extent that he purchased season tickets for each of these major venues, always reserving the identical: Aisle Seat, 3rd Row, Left, Orchestra.

On a number of occasions, an attractive woman named Ruth Feldman, occupied the seat next to him, also alone. At first, they merely nodded "Hellos" to each other. But as time rolled by, they were sitting next to each other more often and conversed more, including exchanging their names. For the first time in years, Ollie felt an emotional attraction when they greeted each other and chatted. He wondered if the attraction was mutual.

His spirit became dampered, however, upon seeing what clearly appeared to be a wedding ring on her left hand. He decided that he needed to know her personal status and would ask her at next week's presentation of the opera "Rigoletto".

Unfortunately, that was not to be. During Ollie's meeting with Frank and Mary the following week, Mr. M called to inform him of a business emergency---the brick ovens were not retaining the required temperatures for baking the pizzas. He had to close the shop and send the student-employees home. Mr. M needed Ollie to return. Before leaving, Ollie gave his opera ticket to Elena.

At the evening's performance at the Opera House, Ruth was surprised to see a pretty young woman, dressed in a fashionably short black MISA dress, coming down the aisle and sitting in Ollie's seat. The two nodded "Hi" to each other as the curtain opened to the sound of applause. At intermission, Mrs. Elena Fernandez Keys left for the foyer to check in with her hubby at home and then to people watch. She stayed there until the lights flickered signaling the audience to return to their seats.

At the end of the performance, the two wished each other a pleasant evening and left.

Ruth drove home wondering who the sophisticated young lady was. Ruth had noticed the wedding ring on her finger and wondered whether she was Ollie's wife? She was surprised at her feeling of despondency and admitted to herself that she was attracted to Ollie. She vowed to ask about his personal status the next time they met.

[ASIDE: Ollie "Truthfully, I am concerned, she is wearing a wedding ring."]

[ASIDE: Ruth "Truthfully, I am concerned, she is young and pretty, sitting in Ollie's aisle seat, and wearing a wedding ring."]

4.

The period stipulated in the sales contract flew by and the National pizza chain exercised its option and purchased the Mom and Pop Pizza Shop business at the premium sales price of $7.5 million. Mr. M and Mr. and Mrs. Fernandez could happily retire.

Mr. M chose to remain in St Augustine. Ollie did his best in trying to convince him to move to Sarasota but to no avail. They had talked about it a number of times during the past year but Mr. M assured his son that although he would be living alone, he would not be lonely. He told Ollie that he had his Italian Opera collection to keep him company and to soothe his soul.

He purchased a 3-bedroom ranch-style house on Dolphin Drive with a patio and cold beer view of the watercraft traffic on the Intercoastal Waterway. The house was ideally located being only a short distance from the Bridge of Lions walkway to the Historic District. There he could attend mass at the Basilica or meet his friends for lunch or dinner at the many fine local restaurants. Mr. M had operated his carryout pizza shop for nearly 30 years and was looking forward to enjoying the relaxed ritual of retirement living. "No, Ollie, I will not be lonely."

The timing of Frank and Mary Fernandez retirement was perfect. Daughter Elena was happily married to a local tax attorney and lived in a lovely section of Sarasota overlooking Sarasota Bay with its picturesque sailboats. Son Ernest, a recent graduate of Duquesne University, had accepted an entry-level analyst position with the Central Intelligence Agency in Langley, Virginia. And Frank and Mary were excited to move into their newly purchased 3-bedroom bungalow in Elena's neighborhood.

Their socio-economic status had a taken a quantum leap from their earlier days living in a subsidized apartment on Orange Street in St Augustine. As Frank eloquently articulated at his celebratory retirement dinner, "you work hard, obey the laws, pay your taxes, and this wonderful country called America rewards you with a quality life." And they decided it was now "give back" time. He and Mary planned to enjoy their retirement years volunteering their services to Sarasota programs for the needy as well as supporting local and national charities. Their initial gift of $10,000 was made to Teach For America, in loving memory of their daughter Rosie.

5.

At the next concert, Ollie arrived early with the hope that Ruth would also. She did, and both greeted each other with warm smiles, happy to see one another. Each was anxious to know the other's personal status.

Ruth quickly took the initiative and mentioned that she was surprised that he had missed the performance of "Rigoletto." Ollie informed her of the business emergency that had occurred prompting his need to return to St Augustine. Ruth then nervously asked: "Ollie, uh...was the pretty young lady who sat in your seat your wife?" "Oh, no, she is the daughter of my business partners. I am single." And when Ollie volunteered that he was single, a relieved Ruth, surprising even herself, quickly blurted out that she was also single.

Ollie seized the moment, and suggested getting together for dinner before next week's performance. To his delight, Ruth was quick to accept and gave him her telephone number and address.

The ritual of romance was about to commence.

The following week, Ollie drove to Long Boat Key, picked up Ruth, and circled back over the Ringling Bridge to "Michael's on East" restaurant for dinner. She looked stunning and he told her so. She was pleased, smiled, and thanked him for the compliment. At dinner, they engaged in a lengthy conversation filling personal knowledge gaps for each other. They learned each experienced a personal tragedy of a loved one. Ollie told her about Rosie and Ruth told him about her husband's fatal accident while on a fishing trip in the Gulf of Mexico. They comforted one another upon hearing their tragedies. They also confided that neither had dated much since. Not, unexpectedly, they soon began seeing each other on a steady basis.

Their personal relationship, which had been cautiously but steadily evolving into a romantic one, moved swiftly once Ruth became comfortable that Ollie was neither troubled by their age difference (He was 27. She was 31.) nor by their religious difference (He was

Catholic. She was Jewish.). A whirlwind of intense personal dating followed. Ruth delighted in showing Ollie the local sights, including the playful dolphins and lumbering manatees at Mote Marine, the world-famous Ringling Circus Art Museum, and the highly-popular Siesta Key Beach with its cool-to-the-touch white, quartz sand. Their evenings were filled attending social events and being with friends and family.

Ollie and Ruth had been seeing each other steadily and had fallen for each other. She enjoyed spending time with the handsome, charming bachelor, and he looked forward to being with the attractive, intelligent widow.

Decision time had arrived.

And Ollie had decided. He knew that Ruth was the life-mate for him and he said so: "Ruth Feldman, I want to spend the rest of my life with you. I love everything about you. Will you marry me?"

Ruth had been hoping for some time that he would ask and was thrilled to accept:

"Ollie Martini, you are exactly the man I have been waiting for. I love you so much. Yes, Yes, I will marry you."

Upon hearing "Yes", Ollie pulled Ruth in close, hugged her tightly, and gave her a long, passionate kiss that literally took her breath away.

Shortly thereafter, Ollie and Ruth were married in an intimate, interfaith ceremony led by Rabbi Gurion and Father Gatto in the Basilica in St Augustine. Witnessing the ceremony were Mr. Martini, Mr. and Mrs. Mel Feldman, Ruth's parents, and the Fernandez family. The religious ceremony was brief with Rabbi Gurion and Father Gatto welcoming the families and guests, co-reading Isaiah Chapter 53 from the Old Testament, and ending with Ollie and Ruth exchanging traditional marriage vows. Rabbi Gurion then informed the gathering he knew Ruth and her family since birth, presided over her bat mitzvah, and of "how proud he was of Ruth's strength and resilience after her personal loss." And Father Gatto recounted to the group his initial meeting of Ollie, the adoption of Ollie by Mr. Martini, and "Ollie's personal growth to the fine young man he is today." Each wished the newly married couple the best, blessed them, and expressed personal joy in their union.

After returning from their honeymoon, Ollie and Ruth settled into a new Bay-side home on the barrier island of Lido Key, furnishing it with love and happiness. Ten months later, they were blessed with a healthy 6 pound baby girl.

Ollie asked Ruth if she had a favorite name in mind for their daughter. "That's an easy one Ollie" she replied "her name will be Judith Ann, in honor of your mother." Upon hearing her reply, a shiver of love tingled through him as he wrapped Ruth tenderly in his arms.

Personal joy had, indeed, returned to their lives.

Mr. and Mrs. Ollie Martini lived happily ever after.

OLLIE AND RUTH
AISLE SEAT, 3RD ROW, LEFT, ORCHESTRA

Once in a while, two lonely strangers
meet by chance
and
Gifts them a fairy tale romance

AUTHOR'S NOTE

This is the first of my Orphan Ollie books.

ORPHAN OLLIE OPTS OUT

In this first book, Ollie, a sixteen-year-old orphan, opts out of his State's program of homes for orphans, and "escapes" to St. Augustine, Florida to attempt to make it on his own.

ORPHAN OLLIE OPTS IN

In stark contrast, the second Orphan Ollie book depicts Ollie heeding the advice of his parish priest and choosing the structured-mentoring home of Boys Town in St. Augustine, Florida.

www.ingramcontent.com/pod-product-compliance
Lightning Source LLC
Chambersburg PA
CBHW071348130626
46556CB00005B/2091